THE BROTHERS GRIMM
Hansel and Gretel

Pictures by SUSAN JEFFERS

Dial Books for Young Readers
New York

Published by
Dial Books for Young Readers
375 Hudson Street
New York, New York 10014

Library of Congress Cataloging in Publication Data
Grimm, Jakob Ludwig Karl, 1785–1863. Hansel and Gretel.
Translation of Hänsel und Gretel.
Summary / When they are left in the woods by their parents, two
children find their way home despite an encounter with a wicked witch.
[1. Fairy tales. 2. Folklore—Germany]
I. Grimm, Wilhelm Karl, 1786–1859, joint author.
II. Jeffers, Susan. III. Title.
PZ8.G882Han   1980   [E]   398.2′1′0943   80-15079
ISBN 0-8037-3492-1   ISBN 0-8037-3491-3 lib. bdg.

The full-color artwork was prepared using a fine-line pen with ink and dyes.
They were applied over a detailed pencil drawing that was then erased.

A Note on the Text
This translation of *Hänsel und Gretel* was originally included
in a collection entitled *Fairy Tales of The Brothers Grimm*
by Mrs. Edgar Lucas, published in 1902
by J. B. Lippincott Company.
The language has been altered only as
necessary to avoid archaic references.

For Dad, Caroline, and Bill

At the edge of a large forest there once lived a woodcutter with his wife and two children. The boy was called Hansel and the girl, Gretel. They were always very poor and had little to live on. But at last a terrible famine came to the land, and the woodcutter could not even provide food for his family.

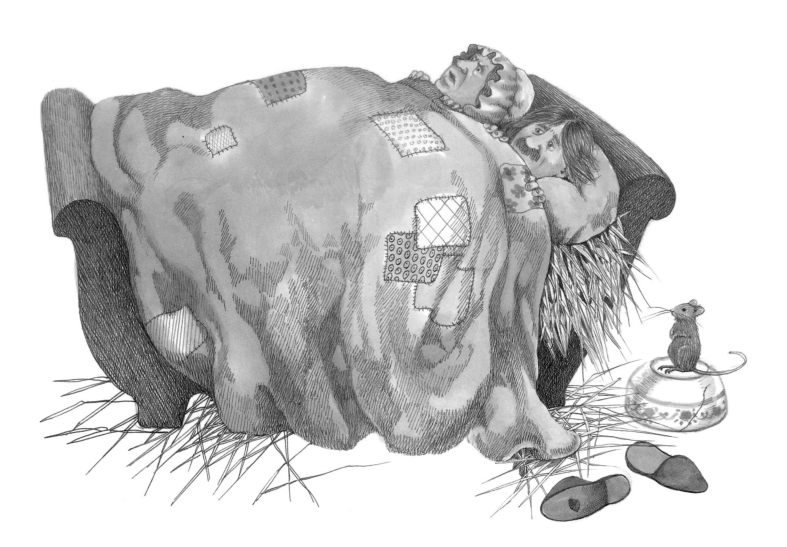

One night he lay awake in bed, worrying over his troubles. "What is to become of us?" he said to his wife. "How can we feed our poor children when we have nothing for ourselves?"

"I'll tell you what," she answered. "Tomorrow morning we will take the children out to the thickest part of the forest. We will light a fire and give them each a piece of bread. Then we will go about our work and leave them there. They won't be able to find their way home, and so we shall be rid of them."

"No, I could never find it in my heart to leave my children alone in the forest," said the woodcutter. "The wild animals would soon come and tear them to pieces."

"What a fool you are!" the woman said. "Then we must all four die of hunger. You might just as well plane the boards for our coffins at once." And she gave him no peace until he consented.

But the two children had not been able to sleep for hunger, and so they heard what their stepmother had said.

Gretel wept bitterly. "All is over for us now."

"Be quiet, Gretel," said Hansel. "Don't cry. I'll find a way to save us."

When the woodcutter and his wife were asleep, Hansel got up, put on his jacket, and slipped out the door. The moon was shining brightly, and the white pebbles around the house gleamed like silver coins. Hansel stooped down and gathered as many pebbles as his pockets would hold.

Then he went back to Gretel. "Go to sleep now," he said. "We will not perish in the forest." And he lay down and slept himself.

At daybreak before the sun had risen, the woman came to wake them. "Get up, you lazybones," she ordered. "We are going into the forest to fetch wood." She gave them each a piece of bread. "Here is something for your dinner, but do not eat it right away, for it's all you'll get."

Gretel took the bread and put it under her apron because Hansel's pockets were filled with pebbles.

At length they all started out for the forest. When they had gone a little way, Hansel stopped to look back at the cottage, and he did it again and again.

"What are you doing?" his father asked. "Take care and keep up with us."

"Oh, Father," said Hansel, "I am looking at my white cat. It is sitting on the roof, saying good-bye to me."

"Little fool!" the woman said. "That is no cat. It's the morning sun shining on the chimney."

But Hansel had not been looking at the cat at all. Each time he stopped, he had dropped a white pebble on the ground to mark the way.

In the middle of the forest where the trees grew dense, their father made a fire to warm them. When it was blazing, the woman said, "Now lie down by the fire and rest while we go and cut wood. We will soon come back to fetch you."

Hansel and Gretel sat by the fire, and when dinnertime came, they each ate their little bit of bread. They thought their father was quite near because they could hear the sound of an ax. They did not realize it was not an ax at all, but a branch he had tied to a dead tree so that the wind blew it back and forth. The children sat so long that at last they fell fast asleep.

When they awoke, it was dark night. Gretel began to cry. "How shall we ever get out of the forest?"

But Hansel comforted her. "Wait until the moon rises," he said. "Then we will find our way."

When the full moon rose, Hansel took his sister by the hand, and they began to walk, guided by the pebbles that glittered like bits of silver.

They walked the whole night through, and at daybreak they finally reached their father's cottage.

"You bad children!" said the woman when she saw them. "Why did you sleep for so long in the forest? We thought you did not mean to come back here anymore."

But their father was glad, for it had hurt him sorely to leave them behind.

Not long afterward they were again in great need, and Hansel and Gretel heard the woman at night talking to the woodcutter. "We have only half a loaf left and when we have eaten that, we will have nothing. The children must go away. We will take them farther into the forest so that they will not find their way back. There is nothing else to be done."

The woodcutter tried to protest, but it was no use. Because he had given in to her the first time, he was forced to agree.

When everything was quiet, Hansel again got up, meaning to go after more pebbles, but the woman had locked the door and he couldn't get outside. Still he consoled his sister. "Don't cry, Gretel. Go to sleep. There is nothing to fear."

In the early morning the woman made the children get up, and she gave them each a bit of bread, but it was smaller than before. On the way to the forest Hansel crumbled his piece in his pocket and stopped again and again to drop the crumbs on the ground.

"Hansel, what are you stopping for?" asked his father.

"I am looking at my dove who is sitting on the roof and wants to say good-bye to me."

"Little fool!" said the woman. "That is no dove. It's the morning sun shining on the chimney."

But Hansel continued to strew the crumbs behind him on the ground.

The woman led the children far into the forest to a place where they had never been before. Again they made a big fire.

"Stay where you are, children," she said. "And when you are tired, you may go to sleep. We are going farther on to cut wood, and in the evening we will come back and fetch you."

At dinnertime Gretel shared her bread with Hansel, for he had left his behind to mark the way. They went to sleep, and the evening passed, but no one came to fetch them.

It was dark when they woke up. Hansel comforted his sister and held her close. "Wait until the moon rises," he said. "Then we can see the bread crumbs that I scattered for a path."

When the moon rose, they started out but they found no bread crumbs. They did not know that all the thousands of birds who live in the forest had swooped down and eaten every one.

"We shall soon find the way," said Hansel. But they could not find it. They walked all night and the next day, but they could not get out of the forest.

They were very hungry, for they had found only a few berries to eat. At last they could not go farther and so they lay down and went to sleep.

When they awoke in the morning, it was the third day since they had left their father's cottage. They started to walk again but they only went deeper into the forest, and they began to fear that if no help came they would perish.

Then at midday they saw a beautiful snow-white bird. It sang so sweetly that they stood still to listen. When the bird stopped singing, it fluttered its wings and flew near them. Hansel and Gretel followed it until they came out into a clearing, and there they saw a little house, wonderful beyond their dreams.

The house was made entirely of cake, and it was roofed with icing. The windows were transparent sugar. The children were so hungry that they did not hesitate at all. Hansel stretched up and broke off a piece of the roof, and Gretel went to the window and began to nibble at that. Then a gentle voice called out to them:

"Nibbling, nibbling like a mouse,
Who's that nibbling at my house?"

The children answered:

> "Just the winds, the winds that blow
> From the sky to the earth below."

All at once the door opened and an old, old woman hobbled out, holding tightly to a cane. Hansel and Gretel were so frightened that the food they were eating fell from their hands.

But the old woman only shook her head. "Ah, dear children," she said. "Come in and stay with me. You will come to no harm."

She took them by their hands and led them into the little house. A fine dinner was set before them, pancakes and sugar, milk, apples, and nuts. After they had eaten, she took them to two small white beds. Hansel and Gretel crept beneath the blankets, and when they fell asleep, they felt as if they were in heaven.

But the old woman who had seemed so kind was really a witch. She had built the cake house especially to lure the children to her.

Witches have red eyes and can't see very far, but their sense of smell is as keen as an animal's, and they know when human beings come close. The witch liked children best of all. Whenever she snared one, she cooked it and ate it and considered it a grand feast.

As soon as Hansel and Gretel were asleep she laughed wickedly. "Now I have them," she said. "They shan't escape me."

Early in the morning, before the children awoke, she went again to look at them in their beds. "They will be tasty morsels," she murmured, gazing at their rosy cheeks.

She seized Hansel with her bony hand and carried him off to a little stable, where she shut him up and barred the door. Though he shrieked at the top of his lungs, she took no notice of him.

Then she went to Gretel and shook her awake. "Get up, you lazybones. Fetch some water and cook something nice for your brother. He is in the stable and has to be fattened. When he is nice and fat, I will eat him."

Gretel began to cry bitterly, but it was no use. She had to obey the witch's orders. The best food was to be cooked now for Hansel, but Gretel had only the shells of crayfish to eat.

Every morning the old witch hobbled to the stable and ordered Hansel to hold out his finger so she could feel how fat he was.

But Hansel held out only a knuckle. The witch's eyes were dim, and she thought the bony knuckle was Hansel's finger and wondered why he did not get any fatter.

When four weeks had passed, she became very impatient and would wait no longer. "Now then, Gretel," she said. "Hurry along and fetch the water. Fat or thin, tomorrow I will kill Hansel and eat him."

How Gretel grieved! As she carried the water the tears streamed down her cheeks. "Oh, if only the wild animals in the forest had devoured us," she cried. "At least we would have died together."

"Stop your weeping! It will do you no good," said the witch.

Early in the morning she made Gretel fill the kettle and kindle a fire. "We will bake first," she said. "I have heated the oven and kneaded the dough. Creep in and see if the fire is blazing high enough now." And she pushed Gretel toward the oven.

The witch meant to shut the door and roast her once she was inside. But Gretel saw what she had in mind. "I don't know how to get in," she said. "How am I to manage it?"

"Stupid goose!" said the witch, rushing up to the oven. "The opening is big enough. See, I could fit myself."

Quickly Gretel gave the witch a push that sent her headlong into the flames, and then she banged the door and bolted it tight.

The witch howled horribly, but Gretel ran away and left her there to perish. She ran to the stable as fast as she could and opened the door.

"Hansel! Hansel!" she cried. "We are saved. The old witch is dead!"

Hansel rushed out like a bird from a cage when the door is opened. They fell upon each other, and kissed each other, and danced around with joy.

There was nothing more to fear, and so they went into the witch's house. In every corner they found chests full of pearls and precious jewels. Hansel filled his pockets and Gretel filled her apron, and then they hurried away out of the clearing.

Before they had gone far, they came to a great body of water. "We can't get across it," said Hansel. "I see no path and no bridge."

"Look there," Gretel told him. "A duck is swimming, and it will help us over if we ask it." Then she sang:

"Little duck that cries quack, quack,

Hansel and Gretel are waiting here.

Please carry us upon your back,

For no path or bridge is near!"

The duck came right up to them, and then it carried Hansel and Gretel across the water, one by one.

As they walked through the forest on the other shore, the trees and hills became more and more familiar to them. At last they saw their father's house in the distance.

Hansel and Gretel rushed inside and threw their arms around their father's neck. The poor man had not had a single moment of peace or pleasure since he had deserted his children in the forest, and while they were gone, his wife had died.

Gretel shook her apron and scattered the pearls and jewels all over the floor. Hansel added handful after handful out of his pockets.

From that time all their troubles were ended, and they lived together in great happiness.